SPECTRA X-PRIME

MantisMan

Strike of the Future

Contents

Prologue

Character Name: MantisMan

Inspiration: Mantis Shrimp (known for its powerful strike and complex vision)

Backstory:

Liam Vega, a reserved marine biology student, becomes the victim of a lab accident involving an experimental fusion of mantis shrimp DNA and advanced nanotech. This unexpected fusion transforms him into **MantisMan**, granting him extraordinary abilities. Now, he must navigate life as both a university student and a superhero, balancing his newfound powers with his quiet, introspective nature.

Powers and Abilities:

- **Hyper-Reflexes:** With lightning-fast reactions, MantisMan can move and strike before anyone else.
- **Enhanced Vision:** His eyes allow him to see beyond the visible spectrum, detecting ultraviolet, infrared, and even subtle energy changes.
- **Mantis Strike:** His signature ability, a devastating punch

with the force of a small cannon.

- **Wall-Crawling and Agility:** MantisMan can scale walls and cling to surfaces, moving with fluid grace.
- **Limited Water Manipulation:** He can control and manipulate small amounts of water for combat and environmental advantages.

Personality:

Shy, intelligent, and deeply empathetic, Liam often prefers solving problems with his mind rather than his fists. As MantisMan, he wrestles with the responsibility of being a hero, while also dealing with the pressures of everyday life. He's quick-witted and self-deprecating, but beneath the humor lies a quiet strength.

Villain:

Dr. Carina Holt, a scientist turned villain, who creates genetic hybrids in her quest to force humanity to evolve for survival in an ever-changing world.

Introduction

Liam Vega never imagined his quiet life as a marine biology student would change in a single night. A brilliant yet introverted researcher, he spends his days studying the wonders of the ocean, fascinated by the raw power of nature. But one experiment, a fusion of cutting-edge nanotechnology and the DNA of the mantis shrimp, goes terribly wrong—and Liam becomes the unwitting subject of the next step in human evolution.

Now, gifted with superhuman reflexes, vision beyond the visible spectrum, and the devastating power of the **Mantis Strike**, Liam must learn to balance the responsibilities of being a hero with the pressures of his everyday life. As **MantisMan**, he fights to protect the city from the dark forces that seek to exploit his abilities, all while struggling with his own doubts about the path he must walk.

With enemies lurking in the shadows and a powerful new villain on the rise, Liam realizes that being a hero isn't just about power—it's about heart, resilience, and the choices you make when no one else is watching. As MantisMan, the future is in his hands.

Chapter 1: The Birth of MantisMan

Liam Vega had always been comfortable in the background. Quiet, introverted, and intensely focused on his studies, he was the type of student who blended into the crowd, even at a prestigious research university. His passion lay in marine biology, specifically in studying the fascinating creatures of the ocean and how their unique adaptations could be used for environmental conservation. It wasn't glamorous, but it was his world, a world that made sense in its ordered chaos.

Every evening, long after his classmates had left the campus for the night, Liam could be found in the university's advanced genetics lab, meticulously running experiments. The lab was his second home, filled with cutting-edge equipment and vials of DNA samples from some of the ocean's most remarkable creatures. His latest research focused on the mantis shrimp, a small but incredibly powerful marine creature known for its lightning-fast punch that could shatter shells and break glass with ease. Liam admired the mantis shrimp's strength and precision, qualities he himself felt he lacked.

One fateful night, Liam was working late, as usual, his mind absorbed in the complex task of fusing DNA samples with nanotechnology. The project was meant to help develop more sustainable environmental conservation techniques, perhaps even giving humans a chance to repair the damage done to the planet's ecosystems. But something went wrong.

As Liam carefully mixed the mantis shrimp DNA with the nanobots, a sudden surge of energy erupted from the machine. Alarms blared, lights flickered, and the lab was thrown into chaos. Before Liam could react, a wave of raw energy engulfed him, sending a searing heat through his body. He gasped, his vision blurring as he was knocked backward into a shelf of equipment. He barely had time to process what was happening before everything went dark.

When Liam awoke the next morning, he was lying on the cold lab floor, the remnants of the explosion scattered around him. His head throbbed, and his body ached, but something was different—he felt... stronger. He stood slowly, his senses unusually sharp. The flickering lights in the lab seemed too bright, the faint hum of the machines too loud, as if his whole body had been turned up to full alertness.

Confused and disoriented, Liam made his way to the nearest mirror. His reflection stared back at him, familiar but... altered. His normally pale skin had a faint shimmer, as if the light was bouncing off of him in odd ways. His eyes, once a dull brown, now glowed faintly with a golden hue.

Panic surged through him as he realized what had happened. The experimental fusion had gone horribly wrong. The mantis shrimp DNA, combined with the nanobots, had somehow merged with his own cells, giving him powers he never asked for.

Liam stumbled out of the lab and into the early morning light. The world outside seemed louder, more vivid. Every sound, every movement, seemed magnified. As he walked through the empty streets, his body felt lighter, faster. His muscles twitched with energy, and before he knew it, he was sprinting down the street at a speed he didn't know he was capable of. He dodged obstacles effortlessly, his reflexes faster than his mind could comprehend.

Panting, Liam came to a halt in an empty alley, his heart pounding in his chest. He stared down at his hands, which still trembled from the adrenaline coursing through his veins. What had happened to him? What was he now?

Over the next few days, Liam's transformation continued to baffle and terrify him. He discovered that his body had developed abilities beyond what he could have ever imagined. His reflexes were now so fast that he could dodge anything thrown his way. His strength had increased tenfold, and he found himself able to leap great distances with ease. His eyes—his once ordinary eyes—had changed too. He could now see in wavelengths of light that no human could perceive, picking up details invisible to the naked eye.

It didn't take long for Liam to realize that he was no longer just a marine biology student. He had become something... more. Something powerful. Something dangerous.

But with his newfound abilities came fear. What if he lost control? What if these powers were too much for him to handle? He couldn't go back to his old life—not with this burden. But what could he do now?

In the weeks that followed, Liam struggled to keep his transformation a secret. He continued to attend classes, though his mind was always elsewhere, always fixated on the strange, terrifying power growing within him. The few friends he had noticed his absence from social events, but he brushed off their concerns. No one could know the truth.

And yet, despite his efforts to remain anonymous, Liam couldn't escape the growing feeling that he was being watched. As his powers continued to develop, he began to sense the presence of others—shadowy figures lurking in the corners of his vision, too quick for anyone else to see.

Who were they? And what did they want with him?

The answer, Liam feared, lay in the hands of Dr. Carina Holt, the head of the genetics project and the brilliant scientist responsible for the experiment that had changed his life forever. Though she had no idea what had happened to him, Liam suspected that she wouldn't stop until she discovered the truth.

And when she did, Liam knew his life would never be the same.

MantisMan had been born, and there was no turning back.

Chapter 2: Reflexes of a Hero

Liam Vega's life had become a blur—quite literally. Ever since the lab accident that fused his DNA with that of the mantis shrimp, everything around him seemed to be moving slower, while he moved faster than he could ever have imagined. At first, his hyper-reflexes were exhilarating. He could dodge cars, weave through crowds, and react to things before they even happened. His body was a finely tuned machine, constantly ready to spring into action. But the constant sense of anticipation made it impossible for him to relax. It was as if his mind was always on high alert.

One day, as Liam was leaving campus after class, he noticed something odd on the construction site near the university's main building. A group of workers were rushing to clear out, and a loud creaking noise echoed from above. Without thinking, Liam's head snapped upward, his enhanced senses immediately locking onto the source of danger—a massive steel beam was teetering on the edge of the half-built building, about to crash down.

Time seemed to slow.

Without thinking, Liam sprinted toward the site, covering the distance in what felt like an instant. He could hear the groans of the crumbling structure above, the workers yelling in confusion as they scrambled to get away. But it wasn't them he was focused on. In the chaos, a group of students—completely unaware of the danger—stood directly in the beam's path, laughing and chatting as if the world weren't about to collapse on top of them.

Liam's pulse quickened. His vision narrowed. Every detail of the scene sharpened in his mind, crystal clear and painfully vivid. In his old life, there was no way he would have reached them in time. But now?

Liam leaped into action.

He darted forward, zigzagging through the workers and equipment. His movements were fluid, instinctive. As he reached the group of students, he grabbed the nearest one by the arm, pulling them aside just as the beam came crashing down. The impact sent a cloud of dust and debris into the air, but the students were safe, shielded behind a stack of metal scaffolding that Liam had managed to pull them behind in the nick of time.

For a moment, everything was still. The students, wide-eyed and trembling, stared at him in disbelief. One of them, a girl with a red scarf, looked at him as if he were a ghost. "Who... how did you do that?"

Liam swallowed hard, his heart still racing. He realized then that his face was exposed—no mask, no disguise. He had just revealed his abilities to a group of strangers. Panic welled up inside him. What if they recognized him? What if they told someone?

Without a word, Liam turned and sprinted away, disappearing into the maze of buildings before anyone could stop him. He moved so fast that by the time the dust cleared and the students could blink, he was already gone.

Back in the safety of his small apartment, Liam paced restlessly, his mind racing. His body was still buzzing from the adrenaline, his reflexes humming with energy. He had saved those people—there was no doubt about that—but at what cost? He couldn't stay hidden forever. Someone would recognize him, or worse, someone would figure out what he was. He had been so careful up until now, but today had been different. The speed, the reflexes—it was all becoming harder to control.

The next morning, as Liam sat in his usual spot in the campus cafeteria, his phone buzzed with a notification. He unlocked it absentmindedly, only for his heart to stop when he saw the headline:

"Masked Hero Saves Students in Near-Disaster at University Construction Site!"

His stomach dropped as he scrolled through the article. A grainy, low-quality video had surfaced, showing the tail end of his rescue. Though the footage was blurry, the figure—a flash of movement too fast for the camera to capture clearly—was unmistakably him. The internet had already started speculating about the identity of the "Masked Hero," though thankfully, no one had gotten a clear enough look at his face. But it was only a matter of time.

Liam groaned and buried his face in his hands. This was exactly what he had been trying to avoid. Being exposed like this—it made him a target. And not just for curious students or local reporters. There were people who wouldn't be so kind, people who would want to use his powers for their own purposes.

As if on cue, his phone buzzed again. This time, it was a message from Nina, his best friend and fellow lab assistant.

Nina: _"Liam, we need to talk. Something weird is going on with Dr. Holt. She's been asking a lot of questions about you."_

Liam's heart sank. Of course, Dr. Carina Holt—the head of the genetics project that had changed his life—wouldn't let his absence go unnoticed. She was brilliant but ruthless, a scientist who pushed boundaries without regard for ethical considerations. If she suspected something, if she was connecting the dots between him and the accident, she wouldn't stop until she uncovered the truth. And if she knew what he had become, what he was capable of...

A cold shiver ran down Liam's spine. He had to be more careful. He couldn't afford to draw attention—not from Dr. Holt, not from anyone. But at the same time, he couldn't just stand by while innocent people were in danger.

Torn between hiding his abilities and the growing responsibility to use them, Liam knew he had reached a crossroads. The accident had changed him, made him something more than human. And now, the world was beginning to take notice.

But was he ready to be the hero they thought he was?

Liam didn't know the answer to that. All he knew was that, somehow, he had to find a way to stay one step ahead of those who would exploit him. His powers were incredible, but they were also a curse—a responsibility he hadn't asked for.

And as he stared out the window at the bustling city below, he couldn't shake the feeling that something darker was lurking just out of sight, waiting for him to make the wrong move.

The reflexes of a hero weren't just about speed. They were about knowing when to act—and when to disappear.

Chapter 3: Through a New Lens

The next few days passed in a blur of unease and strange new experiences for Liam. After the incident at the construction site, he tried his best to lie low, keeping his head down in class and avoiding any attention. But something else had changed within him, beyond the hyper-reflexes and superhuman agility. His vision had started to shift—he was seeing things differently, in ways he couldn't explain.

It started gradually. One morning, while walking to his biology lecture, Liam noticed the colors of the autumn leaves were unusually vivid, the sunlight reflecting off them in sharp, prismatic rays. He blinked, thinking maybe his eyes were playing tricks on him, but it kept happening. The sky, the buildings, even people's faces seemed to shimmer with subtle hues and textures he had never noticed before. It was like the world had gained an extra layer of depth.

Liam decided to test his new sight later that night. After everyone else in his apartment building had gone to sleep, he climbed onto the rooftop, breathing in the cool night air. The city stretched out before him, a web of lights and shadows. He focused, trying to activate whatever this new ability was.

And then it happened.

His eyes adjusted, and suddenly, he was seeing beyond the visible spectrum of light. The buildings took on a strange, neon glow as he shifted through wavelengths of ultraviolet, then infrared. He could see the heat signatures of people moving in their apartments, the faint traces of animals scurrying in the shadows. Beyond that, he could sense energy—electricity coursing through power lines, the low hum of wireless signals pulsing in the air. His enhanced eyesight allowed him to see things that no normal human could perceive.

But there was more. As he gazed across the city, he noticed something unsettling. There was a dark corner near the university that seemed... off. At first glance, it looked like just another nondescript office building, but when he switched to a different wavelength, the building's true nature was revealed. A network of security beams crisscrossed the windows, and the faint outlines of hidden cameras blinked in and out of view.

"What the...?" Liam muttered under his breath.

Curiosity gnawed at him. The building was part of the university's research wing, a section he had never been allowed to access, even as a student in marine biology. What kind of research was being done there? And why did they need such high-level security?

Switching back to normal vision, Liam made a note of the building's location. He couldn't shake the feeling that something was seriously wrong. This wasn't just about his powers anymore—

there was something deeper happening at the university, something hidden in plain sight.

But before he could investigate further, his phone buzzed with a text from Nina:

Nina: _"We need to talk ASAP. Dr. Holt is up to something weird. Meet me at the lab tomorrow night?"_

Liam's pulse quickened. Nina was the only person he trusted, the only one who had any idea that something had happened to him. He had told her bits and pieces about the accident, but he hadn't revealed everything yet. Still, if Dr. Holt was involved, Liam needed to know what she was planning. Holt was brilliant, no doubt, but her methods had always been... questionable. She pushed boundaries, and if she had somehow connected Liam's disappearance with the incident in the lab, she wouldn't rest until she uncovered the truth.

The next evening, Liam made his way back to the genetics lab, keeping a low profile as he slipped through the back entrance. The lab was eerily quiet, the fluorescent lights flickering as he moved down the hall. He found Nina waiting for him near the research station where the accident had taken place. She looked anxious, her dark hair tied back in a hurried ponytail, her eyes darting nervously around the room.

"You okay?" Liam asked, trying to keep his voice steady.

Nina nodded, but her expression was tight with worry. "Liam, I've been looking into Dr. Holt's research. Something's off. She's been pulling data from the military and private contractors—stuff that has nothing to do with environmental conservation. She's hiding something big."

Liam's heart sank. He had suspected as much, but hearing it from Nina made it all too real. "What kind of research?"

Nina hesitated, biting her lip. "Superhuman enhancement. Genetic manipulation. She's been using our project as a front for military-grade experiments. Liam... I think she knew something like this could happen to you. The nanotech, the DNA splicing— it was never about saving the ocean. It was about creating superhumans. You were just an accidental success."

Liam felt a cold chill run down his spine. He had feared this— feared that his powers weren't just a freak accident, but part of something much larger and far more dangerous.

"She's been looking into you," Nina continued. "She knows you've been absent, and she's started asking questions about that night in the lab. I don't think it'll be long before she figures out what really happened."

Liam's mind raced. Dr. Holt was already suspicious, and now it seemed she had been planning something far more sinister than he had imagined. But there was something else bothering him—something Nina hadn't mentioned yet.

"What's in that building?" Liam asked, his voice low.

Nina frowned. "What building?"

"The one near the university research wing. It's heavily guarded, like something out of a military base. I saw it last night."

Nina's eyes widened. "That's one of Holt's black sites. It's where she does her off-the-books experiments—stuff she doesn't want the university or the government to know about. I've never been inside, but I've heard rumors. Dangerous stuff. If she's got something there, it's bad news."

Liam clenched his fists. He had to stop her, but he didn't even know where to begin. His powers were still unpredictable, and if Holt was already on his trail, confronting her directly would be a huge risk.

But he couldn't just sit back and do nothing. Whatever Holt was planning, it involved him. And if she had already started creating superhumans... he wasn't the only one in danger.

Nina put a hand on his arm, her voice soft but determined. "Liam, we have to stop her. I'll help you. But we need to be smart about this. She's dangerous."

Liam nodded, his jaw set. "I know. But we have to move fast. Before it's too late."

As they left the lab, Liam couldn't shake the feeling that they were running out of time. His new powers had given him incredible abilities, but they had also thrust him into a world of dark secrets and dangerous enemies. And now, with his enhanced vision, he could see the threats lurking in every shadow.

Through his new lens, the world had changed. And it was only getting darker.

Chapter 4: The Mantis Strike

The moon hung high above the city, casting an ethereal glow over the labyrinth of streets and alleys below. Liam Vega, cloaked in the shadows of the night, crouched on the edge of a rooftop. His heart raced, not from the thrill of the height or the chill of the evening air, but from the ominous feeling that something was about to happen.

For days now, Dr. Carina Holt's interest in him had taken a dangerous turn. Liam had hoped to stay under the radar, but his brief moments of heroism and increasingly frequent disappearances had drawn the ire of her operatives. He had managed to avoid them so far, but tonight, he could feel the tension in the air.

Suddenly, a group of figures appeared on the opposite rooftop. They wore dark, high-tech suits that shimmered with concealed gadgets and weaponry. Liam recognized the insignia on their chest plates—the same one associated with Holt's research division. His instincts kicked into high gear. They were here for him, and he couldn't afford to be caught off guard.

He leaped from the rooftop, landing silently on the ground below.

The agents were quick to follow, their movements precise and coordinated. Liam's heightened senses picked up every whisper of their conversation, every subtle shift in their stance. They were searching for him, and he had to act fast.

As the agents closed in, Liam made his move. He darted into a narrow alley, using his speed to stay just out of reach. His new reflexes allowed him to weave effortlessly between obstacles, but he knew the real test would be the confrontation. He needed to be prepared for what was coming.

The agents finally cornered him in a dead end. Liam's heart pounded as he turned to face them, his mind racing through the possibilities. His instincts told him to brace himself for a fight. He clenched his fists, feeling the raw power coursing through his veins.

One of the agents stepped forward, their voice muffled by a helmet. "Liam Vega. We've been looking for you."

Liam's response was a low growl. "I'm not going down without a fight."

The agents spread out, weapons drawn. Liam could see the sleek, menacing designs of their gear—advanced tech meant to neutralize threats. He had no choice but to rely on his own abilities. As the first agent lunged at him, Liam moved with blinding speed, evading the attack and countering with a swift kick that sent the agent crashing into a wall.

The other agents reacted quickly, their coordinated strikes

coming from all directions. Liam ducked, dodged, and weaved, his agility a blur of motion. His enhanced reflexes allowed him to anticipate their moves, but he needed more than just speed. He needed to unleash his full power.

With a burst of energy, Liam charged forward, his fists glowing with an intense, crackling force. He had been experimenting with his abilities, and he knew he was ready for this moment. As he swung his fist, he unleashed the Mantis Strike—a devastating punch fueled by the raw strength of his hybrid DNA.

The impact was explosive. The ground trembled, and the wall behind the agents shattered, sending debris flying. The agents were thrown back, their high-tech suits struggling to protect them from the force of the blow. Liam stood amidst the chaos, his breath heavy and ragged.

For a moment, the alley was silent, save for the distant sirens of the city. Liam surveyed the damage, his mind racing. The Mantis Strike had proven to be even more powerful than he had anticipated, and the destruction it wrought left him with a grim realization. His abilities could be catastrophic if wielded carelessly.

The remaining agents retreated, their plans thwarted for the moment. Liam watched them disappear into the night, knowing that this encounter was only the beginning. Dr. Holt's obsession with replicating his transformation would only escalate, and he needed to be prepared for the challenges ahead.

As he stood alone in the wreckage of the alley, Liam felt a mix of relief and unease. The power he possessed was immense, but it came with a heavy burden. He had to control it, master it, and ensure it was used for the right purposes. The city depended on him, and he was determined not to let it down.

Liam took a deep breath and turned towards the skyline, the city lights twinkling like stars in the distance. The road ahead was fraught with danger, but he knew he had to walk it with courage and resolve. The Mantis Strike had marked a turning point in his journey, and now, more than ever, he needed to embrace his role as MantisMan.

Chapter 5: Secrets Unveiled

The next morning, Liam's exhaustion was evident. He hadn't slept much after the fight, and the adrenaline still buzzed in his veins. The city, unaware of the chaos that had unfolded just hours before, bustled with its usual routine. Liam moved through the campus, trying to keep his composure. He had to remain vigilant and discreet, but he also needed to figure out his next steps.

Nina Parker, his best friend and fellow lab assistant, had noticed Liam's increasingly erratic behavior. They'd shared countless late nights at the lab, and she could tell when something was wrong. As Liam entered their shared workspace, she was waiting for him, her eyes filled with concern.

"Liam, we need to talk," Nina said, her tone serious. "You've been acting strange lately. What's going on?"

Liam hesitated. He had considered keeping his transformation a secret, but he trusted Nina. They'd been through too much together for him to keep this from her any longer. He glanced around to make sure they were alone and then took a deep breath.

"I've... changed," Liam said quietly. "Something happened at the lab. I'm not the same as I was before."

Nina's eyes widened. "Changed? How?"

Liam began to explain his transformation, recounting the night of the experiment gone wrong, his exposure to the hybrid DNA and nanobots, and the subsequent powers he had developed. As he spoke, Nina's initial shock turned to disbelief, and then to concern.

"This sounds... incredible, but also dangerous," Nina said, trying to process the information. "You're telling me you have superhuman abilities now?"

Liam nodded. "Yes, and I've had to use them to defend myself. Dr. Holt's agents came after me last night. I'm afraid of what might happen if she gets hold of my abilities."

Nina's expression hardened with resolve. "We need to find out what Holt's planning. If she's after your abilities, there's a good chance she's hiding something much bigger."

The two of them delved into Holt's research files, which Liam had managed to keep hidden in a secure location. Nina's skills with data analysis quickly came into play. She sifted through documents, financial records, and confidential reports. What they uncovered was chilling.

Dr. Holt's research wasn't merely about environmental conservation or the betterment of science. It was a façade. Beneath the surface, Holt had been secretly funded by military interests, aiming to weaponize the hybrid technologies. The documents detailed a series of experiments designed to create superhuman soldiers, each more advanced than the last.

Nina's face turned pale as she read through the information. "This isn't just about your transformation, Liam. Holt was planning to create an army. And if she succeeded, she could use them for anything—war, control, you name it."

Liam felt a surge of anger and betrayal. "All this time, I thought she was working for a noble cause. I trusted her, and now I see it was all a lie."

Nina put a comforting hand on his shoulder. "We can't let her get away with this. We need to stop her before she can do any more damage."

They continued to investigate, tracing the source of Holt's funding and uncovering more about her hidden projects. It became clear that Holt's ultimate plan was to showcase the superiority of her research by unleashing a new hybrid—one that was more advanced than anything Liam had encountered.

With the knowledge they had gained, Liam and Nina prepared to confront Holt. Liam began training rigorously, focusing on mastering his powers and honing his combat skills. Nina, ever resourceful, used her expertise to create strategies and develop countermeasures for the technology Holt might deploy.

As they worked together, their bond grew stronger. Nina's

support became invaluable to Liam, and he relied on her not just as a friend but as an essential partner in his quest to stop Dr. Holt.

The city continued to go about its daily life, unaware of the brewing storm. But Liam and Nina knew that the time to act was approaching. Dr. Holt's ambitions were vast and dangerous, and they had to be ready to face whatever challenges lay ahead.

As the days passed, Liam grew more confident in his role as MantisMan. He had learned to control his powers, understanding their potential and their limits. But the true test was still to come. The final confrontation with Dr. Holt loomed on the horizon, and Liam knew that he had to be prepared for the fight of his life.

With Nina by his side, Liam felt a renewed sense of purpose. He was no longer just a student or a scientist. He was MantisMan, and he was ready to protect his city from the forces of darkness that sought to exploit his abilities.

Chapter 6: Walls and Water

L iam Vega's days as a quiet marine biology student felt like a distant memory. Now, each day was a blend of vigilance, training, and the relentless pursuit of mastering his newfound abilities. His transformation into MantisMan had brought incredible powers, but also an immense responsibility. As he trained, he found solace in the rhythm of movement and the challenge of refining his skills.

One chilly evening, Liam stood on a deserted rooftop, the city's lights below flickering like stars. He was practicing his wall-crawling ability, a skill he'd been developing to its full potential. The process of scaling the buildings with the agility of a mantis shrimp felt surreal but exhilarating. His fingers, equipped with enhanced gripping capabilities, clung to the rough surfaces of the walls as he moved fluidly upward.

He paused midway up the side of a skyscraper, his senses alert to the night's sounds. The distant hum of traffic, the occasional siren, and the occasional chirp of nocturnal creatures were all amplified by his heightened perception. The practice gave him a sense of control and an understanding of his place in the urban landscape—a place where he could blend into the shadows and remain a vigilant protector.

However, as he descended from the building, a new power began to reveal itself—water manipulation. It had started subtly during a particularly intense training session where he was trying to hone his physical agility. He had inadvertently created small, swirling currents of water, and with each experiment, the manipulation grew stronger. Now, standing on the rooftop, he began to test this new ability more deliberately.

Liam extended his hand, focusing on the air around him. Slowly he willed the humidity to coalesce into droplets. The process was challenging; it required concentration and a precise mental command. After several attempts, he succeeded in forming a small sphere of water. It hovered in the air, responding to his gestures. He was able to shape it into various forms—defensive barriers, projectiles, and even a fine mist. It was a powerful tool one that added a new dimension to his combat capabilities.

As he practiced, the sky above him darkened. The moon cast long shadows, and the city below became a maze of lights and darkened streets. It was during this exercise that he heard the faint sound of sirens growing louder. His heightened senses detected something unusual—an urgent energy in the city that suggested trouble.

Liam decided to investigate. Using his agility and newfound water manipulation abilities, he navigated the city's rooftops, blending into the surroundings as he moved. The destination was a district known for its commercial activity, now eerily quiet. As he approached the source of the commotion, his enhanced vision picked up faint, unusual energy signatures—indicative of high-tech equipment.

He followed the trail to an abandoned warehouse at the edge of the district. From his vantage point on a nearby rooftop, he observed a group of individuals unloading crates from a van. They were wearing the same high-tech suits he had encountered before—indicative of Dr. Holt's operatives. This was not a random occurrence; it was part of something more significant.

Liam carefully descended to ground level and approached the warehouse, staying hidden in the shadows. He could hear snippets of conversation through the warehouse's slightly ajar door. The agents were discussing "deployments" and "synchronization," hinting at a coordinated plan involving advanced tech.

Determined to gather more information, Liam slipped inside the warehouse. The interior was dimly lit, with rows of crates and machinery scattered about. As he moved through the space, he saw that the crates contained various experimental devices and components. It was clear that these were intended for further development or deployment.

His attention was drawn to a large screen mounted on one wall. It displayed a live feed of different locations in the city, including several crucial infrastructure points—bridges, power stations, and water treatment facilities. The feed was accompanied by real-time data on each location's security and operational status.

Liam's heart raced. Dr. Holt was planning something much bigger than he had anticipated. It wasn't just about creating superhumans; it was about controlling vital city infrastructure, potentially causing widespread chaos.

He knew he had to act quickly. With his water manipulation abilities, he devised a plan to disable the equipment without alerting the operatives. He created a series of small water barriers and projectiles to interfere with the devices, short-circuiting their operations and causing minor disruptions. It was a calculated risk, but it worked. The machinery began to malfunction, and the operatives scrambled to contain the situation.

As Liam made his escape, he realized the magnitude of the threat Dr. Holt posed. Her plans extended far beyond individual battles or skirmishes; she was aiming to exert control over the city itself. The scale of her ambition was staggering, and Liam felt the weight of his responsibility more acutely than ever.

Back at his hideout, he and Nina reviewed the data he had managed to collect. The information revealed that Holt was planning a major demonstration of her hybrid technology—an event that would showcase her advancements and potentially deploy her tech-based superhumans throughout the city.

Nina's face was set in determination. "We need to get ahead of this. If Holt is planning to use the city's infrastructure against us, we need to find a way to neutralize her control and prevent any further disruptions."

Liam nodded, his resolve steeling. "I'll continue to practice and refine my abilities. The city's safety depends on us, and we can't afford to fail."

They worked late into the night, devising strategies and preparing for the confrontation with Dr. Holt. Liam's training intensified as he continued to hone his water manipulation skills, using them in conjunction with his physical abilities. He knew that the upcoming showdown would be the ultimate test of his powers and his resolve.

As dawn broke over the city, Liam felt a sense of readiness. He had embraced his role as MantisMan fully, and he was prepared to face whatever challenges lay ahead. The city was on the brink of a crisis, but he was determined to protect it, no matter the cost. With Nina by his side and his abilities sharpened, Liam knew that the battle for the city was just beginning.

Chapter 7: The Strike of the Future

The days leading up to the showdown were marked by an uneasy tension. Liam Vega, now fully immersed in his role as MantisMan, could feel the weight of the city's fate hanging over him. Dr. Carina Holt's ambition had become a tangible threat, and every piece of intelligence he and Nina uncovered painted a picture of a looming disaster.

One evening, as Liam and Nina pored over the latest data, Nina's face grew more troubled. "Liam, I've been analyzing Holt's recent activities. It looks like she's about to make her move. The city-wide demonstration is scheduled for tomorrow, and from the information we've gathered, she plans to showcase her new hybrid superhuman, Zero."

Liam's fists clenched. "Zero. The name alone sounds ominous. What do we know about this 'Zero'?"

Nina's fingers flew over the keyboard as she brought up a dossier on the screen. "Zero is supposed to be an advanced hybrid—more sophisticated than anything we've seen. Holt has integrated cutting-edge tech with her human-enhancement experiments. Zero will likely have enhanced strength, agility, and, potentially, tech-based abilities that could disrupt our systems. If Holt unleashes Zero on the city, it could be catastrophic."

Liam's mind raced. He knew that to stop Holt, he would need to be prepared for an opponent unlike any he had faced. "What's the plan?"

Nina looked determined. "We need to disrupt the demonstration and neutralize Zero before Holt can deploy him. We'll need to infiltrate the event, gather as much information as possible, and find a way to neutralize Zero. I've hacked into Holt's security systems and found the location of the demonstration—it's at the city's central plaza, a highly secured area."

The central plaza was an iconic location, known for its grand architecture and as a hub for public events. Securing it would be challenging, but the stakes were too high to ignore. Liam and Nina spent the rest of the night planning their approach, formulating strategies for infiltration, and considering the worst-case scenarios.

The following day, Liam donned his MantisMan suit, feeling the familiar rush of power and responsibility. The suit had become an extension of himself, integrating with his abilities and enhancing his performance. He and Nina approached the central plaza, blending into the crowd as they prepared for the critical mission.

As they neared the plaza, the grandeur of the event site became apparent. High-tech security measures were in place, with guards stationed at every entry point and surveillance systems monitoring the area. The demonstration was set to take place on a raised platform at the center of the plaza, with a large crowd of onlookers expected to gather.

Liam and Nina observed from a distance, using a combination of stealth and technology to assess the situation. Nina deployed small drones to scan the area and provide real-time updates on security and movements. Liam, utilizing his agility and enhanced senses, surveyed the perimeter for potential entry points.

"Looks like Holt has put a lot of resources into this," Nina said her eyes focused on the screen. "We'll need to create a diversion to get close to the platform."

Liam nodded, formulating a plan. "I can use my water manipulation to disrupt the security systems. If I can cause a temporary blackout or system malfunction, it will create an opening for us to get closer."

With their plan in place, Liam and Nina moved into position Liam began by manipulating a nearby water source, sending a controlled flow towards the plaza's security control room. The water interacted with the electronic systems, causing a series of short circuits and temporary power outages.

The security team scrambled to respond to the malfunction, giving Liam and Nina the opportunity they needed. They slipped through the chaos and made their way towards the platform. Liam's reflexes allowed him to navigate through the disarray with ease, while Nina used her technical expertise to bypass locked doors and security measures.

As they approached the platform, the demonstration was about to commence. Dr. Holt stood at the podium, addressing the crowd with a charismatic but chilling demeanor. Her speech was filled with boasts about the advancements of her research and the superiority of her new hybrid technology.

The crowd's excitement was palpable, but Liam and Nina knew that the true threat lay in the introduction of Zero. They watched intently as Holt prepared to unveil her creation.

The moment finally arrived. From behind a curtain, Zero emerged—a towering figure clad in advanced tech armor. The suit was sleek and menacing, equipped with various gadgets and weaponry. Zero's eyes glowed with an eerie blue light, and he moved with a fluid grace that hinted at his enhanced capabilities.

Liam's heart pounded. He could sense the power emanating from Zero, and he knew that this confrontation would be different from any he had faced before. He took a deep breath, steeling himself for the battle to come.

Holt began to demonstrate Zero's abilities, showcasing his strength and agility with controlled displays of power. The crowd watched in awe, unaware of the potential danger that lurked beneath the surface. Liam and Nina knew they had to act quickly before the demonstration reached its climax.

Liam positioned himself strategically, ready to strike. As Holt signaled Zero to begin a more aggressive demonstration, Liam sprang into action. Using his enhanced speed and agility, he darted towards the platform, evading the security personnel and making his way to Zero.

The first clash was intense. Liam's Mantis Strike met Zero's advanced armor with a thunderous impact. Zero's suit absorbed the force of the blow, but Liam could tell that the hybrid was more than a match for him. The fight escalated quickly, with Zero demonstrating his tech-based abilities by manipulating energy and creating powerful shockwaves.

Liam relied on his agility and reflexes to dodge Zero's attacks, using his water manipulation to create defensive barriers and counterattacks. The plaza erupted into chaos as the crowd panicked and security forces tried to regain control. Nina, positioned at a safe distance, provided support by hacking into the security systems and creating distractions.

The battle between MantisMan and Zero raged on, with both combatants showcasing their extraordinary abilities. Liam's Mantis Strike proved to be a formidable weapon, but Zero's tech-based powers disrupted his enhanced vision and sensory perception.

Despite the overwhelming odds, Liam refused to back down. He pressed on, using every ounce of his strength and skill to counter Zero's attacks. The fight took them across the plaza, from the platform to the surrounding streets, as they clashed in a display of raw power and advanced technology.

In the midst of the battle, Liam could see the fear and uncertainty in the crowd's eyes. He knew that he had to end the confrontation quickly to prevent further harm. With a burst of determination, he unleashed a powerful Mantis Strike, targeting Zero's weak points and exploiting the vulnerabilities in the tech-based armor.

The impact of the strike caused Zero to stagger, and Liam seized the opportunity. He pressed forward, using his water manipulation to create a powerful wave that overwhelmed Zero's defenses and disrupted the suit's systems. The advanced tech began to malfunction, and Zero's movements became erratic.

As the battle reached its climax, Zero's suit began to break down. The rogue hybrid's final attempt to regain control was met with Liam's relentless assault. With one final, decisive blow, Liam shattered Zero's defenses and incapacitated him.

The plaza fell silent as the crowd watched in stunned disbelief. Holt, realizing that her plan had failed, attempted to flee the scene. Liam and Nina, exhausted but victorious, knew that their fight was far from over. They had stopped Zero, but Holt remained a formidable adversary.

In the aftermath of the battle, Liam and Nina regrouped, assessing the damage and ensuring that the immediate threat had been neutralized. The city would need to recover from the chaos, but Liam was determined to see the fight through to the end.

As they prepared for the next phase of their mission, Liam felt a renewed sense of purpose. The battle with Zero had tested his abilities and resolve, but it had also strengthened his commitment to protecting the city. With Nina by his side and the knowledge gained from their confrontation with Holt, Liam was ready to face whatever challenges lay ahead.

The city's skyline stretched out before him, a symbol of both the beauty and the vulnerability he had sworn to protect. As MantisMan, Liam was prepared to confront the forces of darkness and ensure that the city remained safe from those who sought to exploit its power. The future was uncertain, but Liam was ready to face it with courage and determination.

Chapter 8: Battle for the City

In the wake of the dramatic showdown at the central plaza, the city was left reeling. The streets buzzed with rumors and fragmented reports of the battle between MantisMan and Zero. Amidst the chaos, the truth of what had transpired remained unclear to the public. Liam Vega and Nina Parker knew that the real fight was far from over. Dr. Carina Holt's plans were still very much in play, and the true extent of the threat she posed was yet to be fully realized.

The aftermath of the battle revealed a city in disarray. Damaged infrastructure, shaken citizens, and disrupted services painted a grim picture of the day's events. Holt's failed demonstration had not only exposed the hybrid technology but had also left a mark of fear and uncertainty across the city. Liam and Nina took this opportunity to regroup and prepare for the next phase of their mission.

Liam had returned to his hideout, the clandestine space he used for training and planning. His body was bruised and battered from the fight, but his resolve remained unshaken. Nina, ever the tech wizard, worked tirelessly to decode additional data they had retrieved from Holt's security systems. The information was both revealing and alarming.

"Holt's not just focusing on Zero," Nina said, her face illuminated by the glow of multiple screens. "I've found evidence of another project, something she's been developing in secret. It looks like she's preparing to deploy more of her hybrids—her goal is a full-scale operation."

Liam's heart sank. "More hybrids? What's her plan?"

Nina scrolled through the data, her brow furrowed. "It appears she's aiming to seize control of key points across the city— power grids, communication hubs, and transportation systems. Her hybrids are equipped to take over these systems, creating a network of control. If she succeeds, she could essentially paralyze the city and assert dominance over it."

The enormity of the threat was overwhelming. Holt's ambitions were no longer just about showcasing her technology; they were about orchestrating a takeover. Liam knew that if he and Nina were to thwart Holt's plans, they would need to act swiftly and decisively.

Their strategy began with identifying and securing the critical infrastructure points that Holt intended to target. The city's power stations, communication centers, and major transit hubs were all potential targets. Liam and Nina mapped out a plan to protect these sites and disrupt any attempts by Holt's operatives to seize control.

Nina's skills were invaluable in coordinating their efforts. She hacked into the city's security networks, creating false alerts and misleading Holt's operatives. Meanwhile, Liam took to the streets, utilizing his agility and water manipulation to patrol and safeguard the critical infrastructure points. His enhanced vision allowed him to detect any anomalies or unauthorized activities.

The days leading up to the anticipated escalation were filled with tension. The city's usual hustle and bustle masked a growing undercurrent of fear. As Liam and Nina continued their covert operations, they encountered sporadic skirmishes with Holt's agents. Each encounter was a reminder of the high stakes involved.

One evening, as Liam was patrolling a power station on the outskirts of the city, he received an urgent message from Nina. "Liam, I've intercepted a communication from Holt. She's planning to launch a coordinated attack tonight. We need to be ready."

Liam's pulse quickened. "Where is she planning to strike?"

Nina's voice crackled through the comms. "The primary targets are the main power station, the central communication hub, and the city's transportation control center. She's deploying her hybrids to these locations simultaneously. We need to intercept them before they can execute their plan."

Liam nodded, determination in his eyes. "I'm on my way. Let's ensure that Holt's plan doesn't come to fruition."

The night was tense as Liam raced to the power station, his heightened senses alert to any signs of intrusion. The facility was heavily guarded, but Liam's enhanced abilities allowed him to bypass security and reach the control room. He encountered a team of Holt's operatives attempting to breach the facility's defenses. With a combination of his agility and water manipulation, Liam engaged in a fierce battle to protect the power station.

As Liam fought off the operatives, he received a notification from Nina. "The communication hub is under attack. They're trying to disable the city's communication systems. I'm sending you the coordinates. We need to move quickly."

Liam's heart raced as he navigated through the city towards the communication hub. The building was a high-tech fortress, but Holt's operatives had managed to infiltrate it. Liam used his water manipulation to create a barrier, allowing him to advance through the facility and confront the intruders.

The battle at the communication hub was intense. The operatives were well-trained and equipped with advanced technology, making them formidable opponents. Liam's Mantis Strikes and water-based attacks proved effective, but the fight was grueling. He relied on his agility and reflexes to outmaneuver the operatives and prevent them from disrupting the city's communication networks.

After securing the communication hub, Liam received another urgent update from Nina. "The transportation control center is under siege. Holt's operatives are attempting to seize control of the city's transit systems. We need to prevent them from causing a complete shutdown."

With no time to lose, Liam raced to the transportation control center. The facility was crucial for managing the city's public transit and logistics. Holt's operatives had already made significant progress in their attempt to take over the systems. Liam engaged in a fierce battle, using his abilities to counteract the operatives' attempts to manipulate the transit networks.

The night's battles were exhausting, but Liam's determination never wavered. With each victory, he felt a renewed sense of purpose. The city's critical infrastructure remained intact, but Holt's operatives were relentless. The clash between MantisMan and Holt's forces had become a city-wide struggle, with each side vying for control.

As the sun began to rise, signaling the end of the night's chaos, Liam and Nina regrouped. The immediate threats had been neutralized, but they knew that Holt's plans were far from over. The city was safe for now, but the fight was ongoing.

Liam took a moment to reflect on the events of the night. The battles had tested his abilities and his resolve, but they had also strengthened his commitment to protecting the city. With Nina by his side and the knowledge gained from their confrontations with Holt, he felt more prepared than ever to face the challenges ahead.

The city's skyline was a reminder of both the beauty and the vulnerability he had sworn to protect. As MantisMan, Liam was ready to confront the forces of darkness and ensure that the city remained safe from those who sought to exploit its power. The future was uncertain, but Liam was determined to face it with courage and unwavering dedication.

As he looked out over the city, he knew that the fight against Holt was far from over. The struggle for control and the battle for the city's safety would continue. But with each challenge, Liam grew stronger and more resolute. The city needed its protector, and MantisMan was prepared to rise to the occasion, no matter the cost.

Chapter 9: The Final Strike

The city's skyline, once a symbol of hope and progress, now seemed like a battleground fraught with tension and uncertainty. As dawn broke after the intense night of skirmishes, the city lay in a fragile state of recovery. Power stations hummed back to life, communication networks flickered with renewed activity, and the transportation systems began to resume their operations. Yet, beneath the surface of this apparent normalcy, a storm was brewing—one that could potentially spell disaster if not addressed swiftly.

Liam Vega, now fully aware of the gravity of Dr. Carina Holt's machinations, prepared himself for what he knew would be the ultimate confrontation. Holt's ambitious plans to seize control of the city's infrastructure and deploy her advanced hybrid technology had been thwarted temporarily, but her desperation made her even more dangerous. The sight of Zero's tech-enhanced power had left a lasting impression on Liam, and the realization that Holt had more hybrids in reserve fueled his determination to end this threat once and for all.

The hideout was a hive of activity as Liam and Nina reviewed the latest intelligence. Nina had managed to decrypt more of Holt's communications, revealing crucial details about the rogue scientist's next move. "Holt's desperate, Liam. She's planning a final assault, and it's going to be her biggest push yet. She's consolidating her forces and preparing for a decisive strike. We have to anticipate her strategy and be ready."

Liam nodded, his focus unwavering. "What's her plan? Where is she going to strike?"

Nina's fingers danced over the keyboard, and a detailed map of the city appeared on the screen. "It looks like Holt is targeting the city's main power grid and data centers. She's planning to cause a massive blackout and disrupt all communications. This would effectively cripple the city, making it vulnerable to further exploitation. Her endgame seems to be a complete takeover, turning the city into a controlled environment for her experiments."

The stakes were higher than ever. Holt's plan was no longer just about showcasing her technology—it was about seizing control and demonstrating the full extent of her power. Liam knew that to prevent this catastrophe, he needed to be strategic and decisive.

The first step was to secure the city's power grid. Nina and Liam worked tirelessly to reinforce the defenses at the power stations, deploying additional security measures and setting up early warning systems. Liam took to the skies, using his enhanced agility to patrol the perimeter and ensure that no unauthorized personnel could breach the facility.

As night fell, the city was eerily quiet, with only the hum of machinery and distant sirens breaking the silence. Holt's operatives, likely preparing for their final assault, were expected to make their move soon. Liam, cloaked in the shadows of the urban jungle, awaited the inevitable confrontation.

The attack came just after midnight. Holt's forces, equipped with advanced tech and coordinated by their leader's meticulous planning, launched a simultaneous assault on the power grid and data centers. The city's lights flickered ominously as Liam received the distress signals from the security teams stationed at these critical locations.

Liam's heart raced as he raced to the nearest power station. The facility was under siege, with Holt's operatives using cutting-edge technology to override security systems and gain control. Liam engaged them with a combination of his Mantis Strikes and water manipulation, creating barriers and projectiles to fend off the attackers. The battle was fierce, with the operatives employing both brute force and technological tricks to breach the facility.

At the same time, Nina worked tirelessly to fend off attacks on the data centers. She used her hacking skills to counteract Holt's attempts to disrupt the city's communication networks. The pressure was immense, but Nina's expertise and Liam's support were crucial in keeping the systems intact.

As the battle raged, Liam noticed a familiar figure amidst the chaos—Dr. Holt herself. She was directing her operatives with a commanding presence, her eyes alight with a fierce determination. Liam knew that confronting her directly was the only way to end this conflict once and for all.

He pushed through the lines of Holt's forces, using his agility and reflexes to dodge their attacks and reach her. The confrontation was inevitable, and as Liam faced Holt, the air crackled with tension. Holt's gaze was cold and calculating, a stark contrast to Liam's resolute determination.

"Liam Vega," Holt said, her voice dripping with disdain. "You've been a thorn in my side, but you're too late. My plan is in motion, and soon the city will be under my control."

Liam's fists tightened. "You're not going to get away with this, Holt. I won't let you turn this city into your playground."

The final battle between MantisMan and Dr. Holt was a clash of ideals and power. Holt wielded her technology with precision, her every move calculated to undermine Liam's abilities. Liam, however, relied on his enhanced strength and agility, as well as his water manipulation, to counteract her attacks and close the gap between them.

The fight took them through the power station and into the heart of the data center. Holt's tech-based attacks were formidable, creating energy fields and shockwaves that tested Liam's defenses. He used his water manipulation to create shields and counterattacks, but the sheer intensity of Holt's assault was overwhelming.

In a critical moment, Holt activated a fail-safe mechanism—a massive surge of energy designed to overload the power grid and cause a catastrophic blackout. Liam could see the energy buildup, and he knew that if he didn't act quickly, the city would be plunged into darkness and chaos.

Drawing on all his strength and resolve, Liam focused his water manipulation ability to redirect the energy surge. With a powerful effort, he channeled the energy into a nearby river, using his control over water to dissipate the surge and prevent the blackout. The city's lights flickered back to stability, and the imminent disaster was averted.

Exhausted but victorious, Liam faced Holt one last time. She was furious, her plans thwarted and her ambitions in ruins. "You may have won this time, MantisMan," she spat, "but this isn't over. There will always be those who seek power, and I'll find a way to reclaim it."

Liam stood tall, his breath coming in heavy gasps. "This city will always have protectors. As long as I'm here, I'll make sure that people like you don't succeed."

With that, Holt was taken into custody, her plans exposed and her influence curtailed. The city began to recover from the turmoil, and Liam and Nina took a moment to reflect on the battle they had fought.

The final strike had been a testament to Liam's growth and resilience. He had faced formidable challenges and emerged stronger, more determined to protect the city he had sworn to defend. As he looked out over the skyline, he knew that the future held both opportunities and dangers.

Liam's role as MantisMan was far from over. The city would always need its protector, and he was ready to face whatever challenges lay ahead. With Nina by his side and the knowledge gained from their battles, Liam prepared for the future with a renewed sense of purpose and dedication.

The city's skyline, once a symbol of uncertainty, now stood as a beacon of hope. Liam Vega had proven himself as more than just a hero; he had become a guardian of the city's safety and integrity. The future was uncertain, but with MantisMan watching over it, the city could face whatever challenges lay ahead with confidence and resilience.

Chapter 10: A New Horizon

The aftermath of the final confrontation had left the city in a state of tentative calm. The chaos wrought by Dr. Carina Holt's schemes had been stilled, and the immediate threat had been contained. However, beneath the surface of this uneasy peace, the city was undergoing a process of recovery and reflection. Liam Vega, having emerged victorious from his battle against Holt and her rogue hybrid Zero, found himself at a crossroads, facing a future that was both promising and uncertain.

The days following the clash were a whirlwind of activity. Dr. Holt's arrest had been the focal point of media coverage, and her plans for a citywide takeover were laid bare for the public. The authorities, now aware of the extent of her ambitions, began to investigate the broader implications of her research. As the media delved into the details of Holt's unethical experiments, the city's inhabitants were left grappling with the realization of how close they had come to disaster.

Liam had returned to his life as a marine biology student, but things were different now. The world he had known was forever changed by his experiences. He had come to terms with his transformation into MantisMan and had embraced his role as the city's protector. The responsibility that came with his newfound abilities was immense, but Liam was determined to use them for the greater good.

The academic world, too, had been affected by the fallout from Holt's revelations. The research community was abuzz with discussions about the ethical boundaries of scientific experimentation. Liam's own research on marine biology and conservation was now seen in a new light, with his contributions to the field gaining recognition for their commitment to ethical science. Despite the accolades, Liam remained focused on his primary mission: safeguarding the city and ensuring that Holt's vision of weaponized hybrids would not become a reality.

Nina Parker, ever the steadfast ally, continued to be an invaluable part of Liam's journey. Her expertise in technology and her unwavering support had been crucial in their fight against Holt. Their partnership had grown stronger through their shared experiences, and their friendship deepened as they navigated the challenges that lay ahead. Together, they worked on creating a framework to monitor and protect against any potential misuse of advanced technology.

As Liam looked out over the city from his apartment, he reflected on the changes that had occurred. The skyline, once a symbol of looming threats and uncertainty, now represented a beacon of hope and resilience. The city had weathered a storm, and while it was scarred, it had emerged stronger. Liam's role as MantisMan was no longer just about fighting villains; it was about fostering a sense of security and trust within the community.

One evening, as he walked through a quiet park, Liam was approached by a familiar face—Nina, carrying a stack of papers and a look of determination. "I've been working on something," she said, her eyes bright with excitement. "I think we need to establish a more formal system for dealing with advanced technologies and potential threats. It's not just about stopping villains; it's about creating a framework that ensures responsible innovation."

Liam nodded, intrigued. "What do you have in mind?"

Nina laid out her plan. "We need to set up a collaborative network that includes scientists, ethicists, and community leaders. The goal is to create a set of guidelines and oversight mechanisms for any research or technology that has the potential for misuse. We can build on the lessons learned from Holt's experiments and ensure that future advancements are used ethically and responsibly."

Liam was impressed by Nina's vision. "That's a great idea. It's a proactive approach that can help prevent future threats before they become crises. Let's make it happen."

The formation of the new framework was a monumental task, but it was a crucial step in ensuring that the mistakes of the past were not repeated. Liam and Nina collaborated with experts from various fields, including ethics, law, and technology, to develop a comprehensive plan for monitoring and regulating advanced research. Their efforts were met with support from both the academic community and local government, reflecting a shared commitment to responsible innovation.

As they worked on the new initiative, Liam also continued his work as MantisMan. His presence was now a symbol of hope and vigilance. He patrolled the city, not just as a guardian but as a figure of reassurance to the citizens. The sight of MantisMan in action was a reminder that the city had a protector who was dedicated to its well-being.

One evening, as Liam and Nina stood on a rooftop overlooking the city, they reflected on their journey. The city was bustling with life, its residents moving forward with renewed energy and hope. The scars of the past were still visible, but they were now symbols of resilience and strength.

Nina turned to Liam, her expression thoughtful. "You know, Liam, it's amazing to see how much has changed. The city is moving forward, and we're making a difference."

Liam smiled, his eyes filled with a sense of purpose. "It's been a long road, but we've accomplished a lot. There's still work to be done, but I'm optimistic about the future. We've created something meaningful, and we'll continue to protect the city and ensure that progress is made responsibly."

As they stood together, the city lights twinkling below, Liam knew that the fight against darkness was ongoing. The challenges ahead were uncertain, but he was prepared to face them with courage and determination. The role of MantisMan was not just about battling villains; it was about shaping a future where innovation and ethics could coexist harmoniously.

The city, now aware of the importance of ethical oversight and responsible innovation, began to embrace a new era of progress. The lessons learned from the battle against Dr. Holt had led to positive changes, and the collaborative efforts to ensure ethical practices were a testament to the city's resilience.

Liam Vega, as both a student and a hero, embraced the duality of his role. He was a guardian of the city and a proponent of responsible science. His journey had transformed him from a quiet marine biology student into a symbol of hope and vigilance. With Nina by his side and a renewed sense of purpose, Liam prepared for the future with confidence and resolve.

The new horizon was filled with possibilities, and Liam was ready to face whatever challenges lay ahead. The city had weathered its darkest hour and emerged stronger, and MantisMan would be there to ensure that its light continued to shine brightly.

Afterword

Dear Readers,

As you close the final chapter of Liam Vega's journey from a quiet marine biology student to the vigilant MantisMan, I hope you've found a sense of inspiration and excitement in these pages. Liam's transformation and his battles against formidable adversaries underscore not just the thrill of superhero adventures, but also the deeper themes of responsibility, courage, and the impact of ethical choices.

Through his struggles and triumphs, Liam embodies the belief that even in the face of overwhelming challenges, one person can make a difference. His story is a reminder that power, whether derived from extraordinary abilities or everyday actions, carries with it the responsibility to act with integrity and purpose.

In the vibrant city that Liam protects, every shadow cast by towering skyscrapers and every light that pierces through the darkness symbolizes the hope and resilience of its people. The trials he faced and the victories he achieved reflect not only the battles of a superhero but also the everyday struggles we all encounter. They remind us that heroism isn't just about grand gestures but also about the quiet, determined choices we make every day.

As you reflect on Liam's journey, consider how you might apply his lessons to your own life. Whether it's standing up for what's right, embracing your unique abilities, or working towards a better world, remember that each of us has the potential to be a hero in our own way.

Thank you for joining Liam on his adventure. May his story inspire you to face your own challenges with courage and to always seek out the light, no matter how dark the path may seem. Here's to the heroes within us all and the endless possibilities that lie ahead.

With appreciation and best wishes,

Spectra X-Prime